BARNYARD
BIG TOP

Jill Kastner

SIMON & SCHUSTER BOOKS FOR YOUNG READERS

SIMON & SCHUSTER BOOKS FOR YOUNG READERS An imprint of Simon & Schuster Children's Publishing Division, 1230 Avenue of the Americas, New York, New York 10020. Copyright © 1997 by Jill Kastner. All rights reserved including the right of reproduction in whole or in part in any form. SIMON & SCHUSTER BOOKS FOR YOUNG READERS is a trademark of Simon & Schuster. Book design by Paul Zakris. The text is set in 18-point Else NPL semibold. Manufactured in the United States of America. First Edition 10 9 8 7 6 5 4 3 2 1

LIBRARY OF CONGRESS CATALOGING-IN-PUBLICATION DATA
Kastner, Jill.   Barnyard Big Top / by Jill Kastner. — 1st ed.   p.   cm.   Summary: When Uncle Julius visits his sisters' farm bringing his Two-Ring Extravaganza along, he livens up everything.   ISBN 0-689-80484-9   [1. Circus—Fiction. 2. Farm life—Fiction. 3. Pigs—Fiction.] PZ7.K1536Ci 1997 [E]—dc20 96-36280 CIP AC

A NOTE ABOUT THE ART

I began with pencil drawings on heavy bristol paper. For this book I experimented with pastel, watercolor, gouache, and acrylic paint before returning to my favorite medium, oil paint. This experimentation with different media gave me a fresh sense of color, which was necessary for this story. After treating the paper so that the pencil wouldn't run or smear, I painted with oils on top of the original pencil sketch. (By the way, the sixth chicken was hiding in the barn. . . .)

—Jill Kastner

For Virginia

Clarence and I were on the front porch racing
Mr. P. and Speedy when Uncle Julius arrived
with his fabulous Two-Ring Extravaganza.

Mr. P. was winning, but we didn't care. In our front yard were two tigers, some monkeys, a lion, acrobats with ponies, a snake charmer with a boa, clowns galore, and three elephants, including a baby elephant named Daisy.

"Holy fazoolis, Gert! It's Julius!" Aunt Ginny whooped.

Aunt Gert came barreling out of the barn. My Aunt G's hadn't seen their brother in years.

Clarence practiced with Pauline and her prancing ponies while Uncle Julius stretched out on the back porch with some lemonade.

"Ben, m'boy, you can keep an eye on things while I visit, can't you?" he asked.

"No problem!" I answered.

I looked at the circus in my backyard. I took care of a whole farm. Running a Two-Ring Extravaganza couldn't be any harder, could it?

Clarence and I woke up extra early
the next morning. There were twice as
many mouths to feed. I did the chores.
Clarence goofed off.

We were running dangerously low on tiger food, so I decided to make a trip to Hinkle's Feed and Supply in town. Clarence promised to watch things while I was gone.

Lucy tagged along, and she wasn't the only one! I began to see that circus talent required more attention than your average farm dweller.

I decided to head home before
we attracted too much attention.

We got there just in time. Clarence swore he didn't know how Bertha ended up on top of the barn.

"Don't we have six chickens?" I asked.

Clarence shrugged.

Clarence was no help that night, either. I swept the barn, mucked the stalls, milked the cows, and groomed the lion while Clarence demonstrated his passing leaps and triple somersaults. He was thrilled that the Flying Freidenhorfs had noticed his exceptional flexibility.

Folks were lining up along the back fence when I fed the elephants the next morning.

Neighbors started dropping by to borrow a cup of sugar or return old tools.

By lunchtime the back pasture was really crowded.

Most of my friends came over, too.
"Boy, Clarence sure has good balance!"
Tommy Zither commented.
Clarence can be such a ham.

All those people poking around started
to make the cows skittish and the chickens
nervous. So when the fire department
showed up, I headed for
the porch.

"Uncle Julius, everyone is getting real
curious about your circus," I said.
Uncle Julius wiggled his eyebrows at
Aunt Ginny. Aunt Gert giggled.

That night the big top was crammed. I think
everyone in town came out to see Uncle Julius's
Two-Ring Extravaganza. Clarence was a hit.

"By gosh, for a domestic, that pig's got talent!"
Uncle Julius exclaimed.

The big surprise of the night came when Uncle Julius introduced the final act: Gertrude and Ginny's Daring and Death-Defying Motorcycle Feats!

I couldn't believe it.

"Who do you think taught me how to run a circus?" Uncle Julius whispered.

The next day the circus
packed up. The big top came
down.
"We're off to Bakersfield!"
Uncle Julius announced.

It hasn't been the same since Uncle Julius's Two-Ring Extravaganza left our farm, but things are getting back to normal.

Besides, Clarence promised to write.